274 Miles

A Scottish Anthology

Tantallon Tìr

274 Miles

Tantallon Tìr

www.tantallontir.com

Published in Glasgow, Scotland in 2025 by Tantallon Tìr.

ISBN 978-1-0682518-0-1

Printed and bound in Great Britain by Clays Ltd, Elcograf S.p.A.

For Jack and Ellen Brennan

"I have sought but a kindred spirit to share it, and I have found such in thee."

– Walter Scott, Ivanhoe

Introduction

Tantallon Tìr was established to fill a Scottish-shaped gap in the literary landscape and through anthologies, novels, and short story collections, we will publish stories by the best writers in Scotland and beyond. Based in Glasgow, the debut publication 274 Miles was chosen to showcase the wealth of talented writers in or from Scotland. Not only does it connect with Scotland in terms of size, with the Scottish mainland being 274 miles long, but with a 274 word limit the writer cannot waste a single word. A difficult task to execute but rewarding for both the reader and writer when done right.

Edgar Allan Poe notes back in 1846 that there is value in being able to read stories in a single sitting, which is something all the editors at Tantallon Tìr agreed with when considering the length of the anthology. Today, brevity is an important aspect of everyday reading, and this anthology suits time-challenged readers who like to read a short story on the bus or train on the way to work and those who like to finish reading a complete work over a few days at most.

We have chosen a balance of stories in multiple genres that complement each other in interesting ways. While the subject matter in a lot of the stories is of a darker nature, both our light and dark stories have depth and say a lot more than the word count provided.

We also have selected fifteen stories containing a form of Scots, all demonstrating how our language can be used to contribute to literature. Whether using Scots or English, the writers produced an excellent piece of work that all four editors agreed to put forward and the list contains some of the best Scottish writers alive today; some are seasoned award-winning authors and best sellers, while others are at the beginning of their literary journey. What they all have in common is that they have produced a story of the highest standard and one that makes this anthology arguably one of the best to ever come out of Scotland.

We had an enormous response for our debut and considered increasing the number of acceptances as the standard was high, but ultimately we stood by the original vision. Thus, what you are about to read is the debut publication of Tantallon Tìr, and I hope you enjoy reading the stories as much as we have.

John Gerard Fagan

Contents

Resolutions

Alan Gillespie

After the appointment the man went home to his wife who was standing in the kitchen with her bare arms crossed over her stomach.

"No luck," he said. "It's still there."

"You should've let me come with you."

"I wouldn't have wanted you to."

She cooked rich dark beef casserole while the man stretched his limbs on the couch. Outside, high wind and rain tormenting the trees. He looked up and noticed something on the wall.

"The calendar needs changed," he said.

"Yes." The woman flipped it up and over onto the next new month.

They ate dinner and shared a bottle of red wine. "What is this?" the man asked. "It's no good."

"It's a Shiraz. It was just cheap. Sorry."

"Just thinking it's maybe time we started getting in a better bottle to go with our meal."

"We can do that, if you like."

Later, as they were lying in bed, the man could not focus on his book. He rolled from one side to the other.

The woman said: "Can you not get comfortable?" Then put her hand on his ribs.

"It's not that."

"Let me know when you want me to go get your tablets."

Eventually she fell asleep and outside the wind died down so that there was no sound. Open curtains and a dark, starless sky. He sat up and rearranged his pillows then lay down again.

In the pitch black of night, she whispered and twitched. The man touched her cheeks and woke her from the nightmare. She curled into him and said his name.

"Are you there?" she needed to know.

"I'm still here."

Nature or Nurture

Lisa Ballantyne

It happened the year the Clyde froze over. I remember the ice groaning. Mum was in the jail and I missed her and the groan of the ice plates over the river seemed to speak what was inside my chest, my heart, yet I was silent. I was fifteen and in care, in a group home. Funny how they call it care – a four-letter word. Not like nurture.

I know his name but I still willnae say it, even in my head. He was one of them meant to look after us. He was younger than the others and thought he was cool. He said he liked me, but he hissed like a snake. Sssss-care. S-care. He got inside me. Under my skin. A skin I cannae shed now.

Now it's my turn to scare him. Spring around the corner and the city has been wild with storms, wind howling through the trees. I know where he lives. Dusk when I cross the park, with a knife hidden. Queen's Park is a Culloden of crocuses. The cycle of nature, of life.

He lives in a tenement – third floor. Not easy to break into, but I'm a burglar now with experience. Stealing started when I was a teenager, shoplifting a cry for help. Nobody heard.

When I ease the window open, I hear he is home. I take after my mum in my personality but she's a tall woman, while I'm petite. I steal inside. I can smell him, and it closes my throat. Inside, I take out the knife. What I'm about to do means I might be inside soon. I dinnae care.

Praying for an Intervention

Seamus Connolly

Blaes pitches. How am Ah meant tae develop ball skills oan such inferior surfaces? Fitba in the pishing rain? Wind blowing up yer hole? Pure freezing wae a Mitre five bouncing aff yer pink legs? Fingers that numb after every game ye cannae button yer school shirt? Fuck this.

We kneel down; me at the single seat across fae Dermot, Mairead beside they two. Ah like the rosary, find it relaxing. Ah don't tell them that, especially they two – Ah'd say fuck all tae them.

The curtains are closed, and the room is roasting with the fire bright red and sparking away. Ah'm jist wearing ma t-shirt and shorts. Dermot's in his Icelandic jumper. He'd suffer for that later – hell mend ye. Dermot always tries tae put me aff – giving me the finger or making dickhead motions from his spotty forehead. He thinks he's funny the thick fucker.

Mum always says tae think ah someone in need of an intervention. So, Ah pray for the manager. Then ah realise Ah'm going bout it aw wrong. There's nae chance Holy Mary would help oot when Ah say – Loving Mary, make that weirdo fucker play me from the start oan Saturday.

Sometimes, daein the rosary Ah hink mad hings like – who does Holy Mary pray tae? Does she pray tae her boy for help? Or does she just go tae Jesus and say – Jesus, kin ye help me? Ah need a haun wae this, any chance, Son?

Dermott was snoring away. Mum looked disgusted; he'd be getting it once we're finished.

"Let me lead this decade, Mum," Ah whisper. She smiles at me.

Harry this Harry that

Rachel Carmichael

He is nondescript yet always there. Offering a brew. Maybe that's what it comes down to, finding someone who will put the kettle on for you, and follow through with the cup of tea.

"Go and help Harry, love," she says.

With what, I want to ask, it's only tea and biscuits. His clogged pores?

Coy when she says she has something to tell me, playing with her pendant. I remove the things I'd left in my old room to make way for his desk and trouser press and a rail of gingham shirts. He is long retired and she knows my flat is tiny.

"What does he do at the desk?"

"All our admin," she says. "He keeps on top of everything."

She puts a framed photograph of Dad and one of Harry's late wife on my old chest of drawers, arranged so they could see each other if they glanced sideways. I ask her whether that's appropriate.

"They would want us to be happy. That's what a good marriage is all about." She gives me the look. "You still have time."

"For what?"

"You still have time. Look at me and Harry."

She isn't rubbing it in, not exactly.

Which one would take care of you. How to tell. They can't all turn into kindly old men.

"Need a hand, Harry?"

A ladybird is struggling on its back on the kitchen windowsill. I coax it upright by its pretty shell and it sways on eyelash legs, unaware of its giant saviour.

"All under control," Harry says, setting out three KitKats.

He swipes the ladybird into the sink and smiles. "Dirty little fuckers."

A Cocktail of Death

Morgan Cry

The walk is a short one. One hundred and twenty-six steps. In the rain. From the car park behind the beach of Fraserburgh Bay to where the man lies. To where the murdered man lies. In a tunnel. A tunnel through which a miniature railway ran decades back. Where the train and carriages used to be stored at night. Where, if you listen, you can still hear the excited screams and shouts of kids ringing around the metal clad walls. Where, only a few hours ago, there was more screaming. Only that wasn't an echo of the past, and it wasn't children.

The seventh to die in seven months. Arms and legs amputated. Head removed. No ID. No forensic evidence found, save a handwritten note on each man. Attached to their left nipple. Pinned there by a safety pin.

The detective pulls on blue latex gloves, leans down, touches the note, turns it over to read it. He knows what it will say. The handwriting is copperplate, probably a right hander, probably by someone well educated, or maybe someone who can only do two things well in life – write and kill.

The detective reads the note.

1 oz. rye whiskey

3/4 oz. gingerbread liqueur

1/2 oz. fresh-squeezed lemon juice

1/4 oz. sweet vermouth

1/4 oz. maple syrup

1 dash aromatic bitters

1 dash orange bitters

It is signed, 'The Mixologist'.

"Is it him?" asks the man with the detective.

"Yes," DI Anderson says, sighing. "Same note."

"It's a weird name?"

"What is?"

"The name of that cocktail."

"You don't say!"

"I mean, who knew there was a cocktail called Can't Catch Me?"

A House of Ill-repute

John Dean

The Reverend Daniel Gallen sat in the armchair and surveyed the girl. She had been the first fallen woman he had met, and it had been a confusing experience for the naïve young vicar in his first parish. The more he learned about Anna, the less he was inclined to condemn her. As he looked at her tight T-shirt, short skirt, and black fishnet stockings, he could see why she attracted men, but had not the Lord Jesus taken an understanding view of harlots?

Gallen first met Anna when he set out to visit an ill parishioner and called at the wrong address, stumbling into a house of ill-repute.

As he listened over the months to the girls' accounts of abusive fathers and cruel partners, Gallen felt even less inclined to judge them, even though they rejected his entreaties to give up the game and embrace the way of the Lord.

He particularly liked Anna and, over time, had to admit that he had fallen in love with her. Gallen even considered quitting his job but resolved instead to ask her to move in with him, saving her from the greasy, lecherous men who called at the house.

On the day he decided to tell Anna how he felt, he found her alone. He was unsure how she would react but of all the scenarios he had imagined, the one he did not expect was mockery.

So, it was that the police found the Reverend Gallen waiting for them, next to her strangled body.

"I think you'd better come with me," whispered one of the officers, leading him out of the bedroom.

The Good Knife

Alan Hay

It was a fine day in early spring, so we took a table outside. He went to the bar and asked if I would take a pint but I was off the drink then so I asked for a coke.

We watched the ordinary people passing by, going about their day, and we talked about the football and the horses and so on until the conversation withered and died.

"I've still got it," he said.

I didn't know what to say to that – I'm not his therapist. I was just trying to keep him going.

"Fuck off," I said, "why would you keep it?"

"It's a good knife," he said. "I use it to cut the bread for my pieces."

He'd grown a beard to try and hide it.

"You never did that with a fuckin bread knife," I said.

Maybe he did, I don't know. I just can't imagine someone doing that to themselves with a bread knife, y'know? I can't imagine that.

I said we'd go away for a few days in the summer. I thought that would give him something to look forward to – just to keep him going.

I never saw him again. Two months later, he borrowed a ladder from his neighbour and hung himself from a roof beam in his loft.

He wasn't my responsibility – there were people closer to him that could've helped.

When I found out, I went to see the neighbour and asked him what the fuck was he thinking? Giving him a ladder? He said he'd told him he was decorating, and how was he supposed to know? He was only his neighbour.

Takkin Flicht

Ross Crawford

Wurd spreidit like wyldfyre through the mercat cross, hooses, and pubs that "ane burdman" wis aboot tae flee fae the waws ae Stirlin Castell thon verie moarnin.

Onluikers suin thranged the castell ramparts, beggars alangside coortiers, thon anticipatit spectakill actin as ane greit leveller the likes ae quhilk widnae be seen again until the battell ae Flodden sum sax years hence.

Froiths of fantasy and imaginatioun amang the crood causit mony tae foirsee sum beistlie mangrel or chimera, beaked and taloned, and they wur thus disappointit by the sicht ae ane smaw and swidderin auld man lashin himsel intae widden wingis daubed wae fithers. Ithers kent this man by nem and reputatioun: John Damian, Italian alchemist, favourite ae the kinge. Ane frawd, sum say. The devill, quhispurt ithers.

Fur his ain pairt, the burdman's resolve hud faltered the seecont he steppit oantae the ramparts. He wis determit tae prove the naysayers wrang, those quho tittill ahint his back and scorne his gyftis. But he'd wantit mair time tae prepare. He glisked at the fithers steekit tae the widden frame, ilka wan pluikit fae plump poultrie. Not the array ae eagill pinions he hud imaginat.

An impatient roar fae the assembled thunnered agin the cobbles and setts, almaist stertillin the burdman fae his perch.

He tippered towart the edge. The widden wings granked. Loose fithers blawn unglewit jouked in the air abone the toun and fermlands, afore disappearin amang the cloods.

"See you in France!" craiked the burdman but ane snell gust fae Braid Street smoored the soond.

Saffron shafts ae licht split the sky ahint the Lomond Hills as the burdman lowped intae nuthin.

Shooder Flesh

Dickson Telfer

Ivry day he begs me fur babies, bit thur's nae point cos the marriage is ower; he jist husnae accepted it yit.

That's whit she said tae me, standin in the tea room nixt tae the sink, shooders touchin, jist so we could huv some form o physical contact. Holdin hands wis too dangerous, ye see, in case somebdy walked in. Wi this plan, naebdy would suspect a hing; we'd jist look like we wurr huvin a blether as we washed oor cups.

Sometimes Ah didnae listen tae whit she wis sayin – no because Ah wisnae interested, Ah wis jist distracted, imaginin the fabric o oor uniforms wisnae there, shooder flesh tae shooder flesh. Made me tingle jist hinkin aboot it. Dinnae git me wrong, it's no like oor skin hudnae touched afore, nor huv Ah goat a shooder fetish, Ah jist desperately wanted tae hold her in ma airms, herts singin, nae claes an nae consequences.

The wait wis excruciatin. Ah'd awready split wi ma girlfriend an gone through the greetin in the shower phase, grievin the loss o somebdy Ah loved bit didnae see a long-term future wi. Bit marriage is different gravy. Mortgage oan a semi-detached villa in Kilsyth in the mix anaw.

That day, as we parted ways, cups left gleamin, Ah walked awa wi a big smile oan ma coupon, cos she'd said it hursel: *the marriage is ower* – bit as Ah goat back tae work, that smile faded. *Ivry day he begs me fur babies* kept playin oan a loop. *Begs*. Ah started tae feel that wey when ye cannae find yer keys.

Christ, whit huv Ah done?

Night of the Damned

Anjali Ramayya

She's drunk already. And mean.

Drink does that to her, they say, thinking it makes you feel better. More forgiving. It doesn't.

You can barely remember a time when she wasn't drunk. Or mean. Maybe when you were five or six. Before the man you called Dad left for work one day and never came back. She'd sat up all night, waiting for him – phoning, texting, chain-smoking.

Cursing you for being born. Ruining her life. Driving him away.

She grabs another pack of beer from the kitchen, slumps onto the settee, and switches on the TV. You ask if she's eaten. She swears, flicks her cigarette stub at you, and turns the volume up full blast. You shrug and retreat to your room. Best to keep out of her way when she's in this mood.

You sit at your window, watching the stragglers spilling out of the pub below, the last bus, the fox skulking near the bins. The street falls silent. But sleep is impossible with the racket from the TV.

You decide to go for a walk. You like walking in the early hours of the morning, when the city shuts down and the only people about are loners, insomniacs, and the damned.

She's lying asleep in an untidy heap on the sofa. The place reeks of piss and puke and singed polyester. A wisp of smoke curls up from the debris of cans, empty wrappers, and fag ends littering the floor.

All you want is to get out.

You grab your coat and backpack from the hall closet, close the front door behind you, and walk into the night.

No People Nearby

Iain Allan Mills

The disappeared often brought dirt into the house during childhood. Soil was always shunned, cleared away, destroyed. Now, Dahlia knows it's a lighthouse. She keeps a little of that dirt around her neck, in a vial painted turquoise, so she might never sail completely into the forgotten. The dirt, a promise of land.

She's only a little thing, Dahlia, but she has these big beautiful blue eyes. Wells of light walled in by intricate petitions designed to degrade all the happenings around her still growing frame. She's beginning to understand.

The cleaner lets her into school when she arrives and she waits, completing homework or studying in one of the plastic rooms. Breakfast club rolls around. The school day. After school club. Scouts. Then, finally, home to dinner, sanctioned leisure and eventually sleep, and release to dream. There are no people nearby.

One afternoon Dahlia danced through the exit gate at Glasgow airport, the add-on for a group of early forty-somethings pre-occupied with their approaching drunken haze and wedding reception. Dahlia, with her big coat on, faux fur collar, Ugg boots, llama hat and mittens waltzed away from the group towards those unseen as the others wheeled away towards the welcoming charms of Glasgow and her cab drivers.

"Sorry... I'm listening to my Metal," Dahlia announced as she withdrew her earphones and feigned surprise that the disappeared might be at the airport to greet her, as if by some inexplicable magic. Delight coloured the arrivals hall as Dahlia brushed off the offer of an embrace and trotted out to the black, tired, but patient Nissan. The footwells were painted with soil and light.

Checkmate

Michael Anthony Fagan

Daddy makes his bed for the final time. Downstairs in the livingroom lies the new Glasgow Charger Chess Club champion 1988. A cadaver in a jacket four sizes too big. Granda stands over him, imagines young Darragh's mind firing at 2,000 miles per hour, careful as a comet, roaming the galaxy in this pathetic bamboo coffin.

Ah shoulda been there, Ah woulda kept ye safe. Ma best wee boy.

At his other side Granny croons, "I watch the sunrise". They clench hands.

In the kitchen, there is only one light – the Glasgow Garden Festival highlights play on a black and white TV as Uncle Brendan drinks his last Lager Lovelies can, feeding a chippy chip to Hamish every time he barks. He thinks of poor Darragh – he's had his chips.

The men in black take him into St Mungo's chapel for his overnight stay. Granda follows behind in his red Ford Fiesta. He plays over in his mind asking Father Mullins if he can sleep up the back on a pew so the boy isn't left alone. If Father says it's not the done thing he'll tell him he is good friends with Bishop Dempsey.

Come on, Father, he's just a wee boy. He cannae be left alone in a big freezing building. He's no even got a winter jacket for Christ sake.

Mammy knits on the couch, chain smoking past the ink, somehow hoping to hear his voice. Margo will be due back from Greece in four days; they have no idea what hotel she's in.

Miss yer wee brother's funeral, ya stupid cow.

Daddy makes his bed, again, for the final time.

Daft Cow

Michele Hinchliffe

Maisie stood and buttoned up her trenchcoat.

"Bye, Mammy."

"Bye, hen. You watch gaun up that road now."

You watch. Maisie thought of Agnes Cooney's murdered body found only weeks before, spitting distance from her house. She shuddered and headed out into a dank February evening to make her way home through the terraced streets of Caldercruix village.

Outside, the big sky was a deep mauve bleeding into grey black and the frozen smoke of coal fires hung in horizontal lines across the windless roof tops.

Maisie turned onto her street, Moss Avenue, which backed onto quiet miles of farmland dotted with pyramidic shale bings. The distant lights of the Black Hill transmitter rose and hung like a string of glinting rubies in the starless night.

She became aware of faint footsteps behind her. She quickened her pace a little, careful not to betray any concern. *You watch*, her mammy's words still in her ears. The steps drew closer, and

Maisie noticed they had an odd sort of scuffling gait. They closed in. Heavy breathing, so close its rank sourness dried her tongue. She gulped as she reached her front gate.

Holding her breath, she turned around. Under the spotlight of the streetlamp, in a plume of frozen breath, she laid eyes on her pursuer.

There in front of her, the murderous fiend she feared was chasing her was, in fact, just a cow, and a young one by the looks of it. The gormless creature stood staring at her, breathing through its nose. Maisie laughed, sighed, and closed the gate behind her.

Daft cow.

#274

Rob McClure

I'd always dreamed of having a wee horse farm, of country peace. How nice it'd be tae sit oan a porch wi' a nice cigarette and a coffee cup and jist listen tae the horses blawin' in the pasture. The turbine man says aw I'd hear is this light whoosh. But right awa', I cannae sleep a wink and can hear its blades popping and knocking, the dug barking at it tae beat the band. A dug kens.

In spring, storms roll through and the trees take a beating. But #274 never stops, jist spins faster, dumb and cauld. Iced up at Christmas, it makes a grinding like it's breaking apart and I'd wish it wis so. I'd think I wis having a stroke! Mah eyes wid flicker this world fuzzy roon the edges.

At night I'd fill the ashtray tae the brim, chew mah wallies till the gums bled. Then the doctor shows us the X-rays and says lung tumors, and I swallowed the yellow pills that made me sick as a dug and got up in the wee sma' hours tae stare at yonder bone-white stalk, its tip emitting red light blinks like some great lonesome smoker in the dark. Aye, there is the doon-drag.

Noo I huv mah country peace, except on windy days when I can hear that far-off creak, and mah dreams (for dreams don't die in the grave, for in here there's only time for dreaming) are of horses whinnying across a green pasture and big white wings that come swooping doon and drag me up intae that rope of cauld black stars.

With the Rising Moon

J. Grobbelaar

The moon's silver glow reflected on the snow, revealing gaps between the leafless trees.

"Where is it? Where is it?"

He swung his arms with force, picked up speed, running onward. He tripped and landed hard on his knees. Scrambling, he threw himself forward. A fire spread through his leg, making him stumble.

"Not now, please, please..."

With clenched teeth, he pushed his aching body towards the rising moon, its glowing body lifting over the trees.

"Where is it?"

As if in answer, the trees opened to reveal a grassy slope. He skidded to a stop just before the slope dropped. The moon bathed the distant valley in a soft, dim light.

He dropped his backpack. Opened it with numb fingers. He swore as the rod got stuck. Trees crashed behind him. Hissing came closer. A foul smell permeated the air.

He gave the rod one last mighty yank. It came free. He dove off the cliff, pressing the button. The device rattled. His hands cramped, holding on.

The glider's wings extended and opened with a jerk. The wings caught the air with a soft tug. He took a deep breath. The cold air made his exhausted lungs burn. He looked back and grinned at the silhouette pacing the edge of the slope, its roar filling the night.

"Not this time, my friend," he said, feeling the weight of the treasure in his pocket.

He turned the glider towards the moon and headed home.

The Working Breakfast

Ricky Monahan Brown

A sister and brother sat at the ends of a long table.

"May I have the toast, Sister?" the man asked.

"Certainly," the sister replied, beckoning the maid to deliver the rack of toast to him.

While waiting, the brother reflected on his intention for the day.

"Today, I will write my masterpiece, depicting the history of an entire civilisation, from the day the earliest of its creators' ancestors crawls out of the sea to the day the last of their descendants perish amid fire and brimstone."

The sister congratulated him on his ambition.

"However," she warned, "I once embarked upon such a project. It is the work of more than a day."

"Maybe that is for the best, for I am possessed of a great apprehension that to create this work would be to call it into corporeal existence, with all the joys – and woes – that would entail, whether in this dimension or the next."

"The next dimension?"

"Indeed. Consider these two slices of toast. This one is our universe, and we dwell as marmalade upon its face, quite unaware of the existence of this second slice of toast, or universe. Now consider the toast rack, and the faces of seven further slices of toast each unaware of the others' existence."

The sister considered this demonstration.

"If your work might call into existence a whole new civilisation and subject it to a fearful apocalypse, I suggest that you retire to bed and do no harm."

Satisfied with his erudition, the brother pushed his work aside and took a bite of toast, heedless of the destruction, tearful goodbyes and howls of anguish he provoked.

Les Maîtres Du Temps

Thomas Welsh

Eight o'clock, ten o'clock, twelve o'clock, one. For time beyond reckoning, the scientist had worked on the Kraznikov Tube in his bedroom, and now it was complete. Taking a step back, he let out a long breath and steeled himself. The calculations resolved, the core already whirring into action. The main edifice was constructed. He could step through any time. A large archway, Einstein-Rosen welded in cold, hard steel.

Time in back go didn't you? Because time in back go can't you?

Dammit, what did it *mean!?*

He glanced at the final note sketched out in shaky handwriting at the bottom of the page. No matter how he tried to ignore it, *that* message haunted him. The earliest version of his machine had allowed simple telegrams to go back and forward on what he called "The long vibrating possibility line of my fate." The entanglement of the quantum states allowed the telegraph receiver to click out its message, and though the quality of the signal was clear, the content of the message was not.

Snapping the notepad shut, he swallowed through a hard knot in his throat, knuckles clenched till they turned white, hands shaking. He could ruminate on this meaningless message no longer! Forcing calm upon himself, Madeleine's smile came to him. So peaceful, so gentle. So out of place in this ugly world.

"No more." As he spoke the words aloud, he cast the last of his trepidation and doubt aside. To Hell with Grandfather Paradox! He pulled the lever. Stepped through the archway. Les Maîtres du temps. The clocked ticked backwards, backwards… wait… *BACKWARDS!*

Too late, he was gone.

Twelve o'clock, ten o'clock, eight o'clock, none.

Tae Never Return

John Gerard Fagan

The school cafeteria wis awash wae screamin n wet laughter. Paddy tasted an acidic rise ae vomit. He swallowed n gripped his bag. The mornin wis oer n he'd survived. Jist a few mair hoors tae navigate. Mammy said it wid get easier. Today wis the wurst it wid ever be. Jist smile n you'll make pals.

He found an empty seat by the windy, away fae the crowds. A voice drowned oot the others.

"Haw, bawbag, you new here? That's ma fuckin seat. Move!"

Before he could react, a can ae cola cracked the side ae his heid n soaked his face. He got up but hauns pushed him back intae the chair.

A puffy girl wae a greasy face wis standin oer him. "You owe me a can, ya prick. Benny get oer here right fuckin now!"

A bigger boy wae glasses sighed n rose fae another table n hauled Paddy oot intae the playgroon by the hair.

"Fuckin stealin juice fae ma bird eh?" he screamed as knuckles n kicks rained fae au angles backed by a squealin crowd.

He wis dragged by three ae thum through a 'no entry' sign tae a disused PE buildin n stuffed intae a rusty locker. Couldnae even move his legs. He stayed quiet as they laughed n chucked broken bottles.

As a distant bell rang, they departed. He tried tae push the door but hud nae strength fae the angle he wis squeezed intae. He cried oot tae silence. They'd come back n get him soon. They widnae jist leave him.

The buildin wis demolished three summers later. The locker wisnae opened ever again.

The Scottish Problem

Douglas Thompson

I was the youngest of four sons. When my mother left hospital after giving birth for the first time, she went to clean out the grate and make the fire for the first time since coming home. She found that my father had written the words 'I love you' in the ash, for her to find there. He had been incapable of conveying this message to her verbally.

A mysterious black bottle sat at the back of our fridge the entire time we were growing up. It must have been there since I was first old enough to stand, walk, and look in the fridge, and stayed there until I was in my late teens. We were told it was a bottle of something called champagne and could only be opened when there was an occasion to celebrate.

Therefore, we have to imagine fifteen subsequent years of birthdays, Christmases, children growing up to be accepted for university, graduating three years later, starting their first jobs. We have to imagine all of that alongside the tacit implication that none of these were deemed worth celebrating.

So what could it be that finally caused the famed and legendary bottle to be opened and a glass poured for each of the family? I'd like to think it might have been my parents' wedding anniversary, some significant number like forty, but unfortunately I really don't remember. What I do remember is that the champagne tasted hideous and had to be poured away before even a drop had passed our lips. It had gone off, because unlike whisky or fine wines, champagne, I was then told, does not keep.

Redwood Reverence

Kate Peel

The path is so overgrown that I almost miss it. The rumble of cars and sporadic *ting!* of clubs connecting with golf balls disappears as I follow the trail into the woods. My soundtrack becomes a robin's song, the rustle of leaves dancing in the wind, the River Doon's gentle babbling. I walk along the river, imagining I'm the first intrepid explorer in an untamed wilderness, when something catches my eye.

There, at the bend in the path, stands the most enormous tree I've ever seen.

The flared trunk spans wider than my outstretched arms. A soaring overstory of conifer reaches so high into the sky that I struggle to fit the whole tree in my field of vision without getting dizzy.

Beside the towering giant, I feel tiny. Inconsequential.

I place my hand against the soft, red bark and feel a thrum emanate from deep within the tree's heartwood. For a moment, we're connected. Acquainted. *It's enchanting to meet you, giant sequoia.* I'm humbled by what this ancient sentinel has borne witness to over the generations. A silent observer to history, change, and time.

Removing my hand, I linger in kinship with my fellow North American transplant. Half a world away from where it started, but quietly thriving in Scotland: a living portrait of strength, enduring beyond, and despite, human reach.

Our encounter may be a mere footnote in the tree's story, but I slip out of the forest forever changed. Stepping onto the street, I glance behind. The pathway blends back into the brush, waiting for the next time it can share this natural wonder in the beating heart of Alloway.

Family Circle

LG Thomson

The triangle held court at the party thrown in his honour, his manner genial, his eyes twinkling as his wife, a smiling circle, served drinks and home-made canapes.

The female shapes noted the triangle's broad shoulders and slim hips. They turned to goo when he spoke to them. The way he focussed his attention made each of them feel like the most fascinating shape on the planet.

Meanwhile, their male counterparts cast appreciative glances at the circle's curves and observed how attentive she was to the triangle's needs. They gave their own rather less acquiescent shapes the side eye, inwardly sighing as the circle refreshed their glasses.

Jealousy aside, everyone agreed that the triangle and the circle made the perfect couple. Everyone knew nothing, for when they departed, the triangle's eyes calcified, and the circle cleared up alone.

That night, the triangle stood on the circle's legs while she was sleeping. She woke up screaming. He told her to get an abortion. The circle cried herself to sleep, and when the triangle did the same thing the night after that and the night after that, she cried herself to sleep again and again, but even although her legs were bruised black and blue she did not yield.

When the circle gave birth to a rhombus, everyone said he had his father's twinkle, his mother's smile. Everyone said that the triangle, the circle, and the rhombus made the perfect family. Everyone was clueless, for each night the rhombus lay in bed listening to the circle scream while the triangle stood on her legs. His smile redrawn as a grim line. His eyes consumed by darkness.

Prawn Korma

Liam McLeod

For breakfast, I ate a fuzzy curry that had been in the fridge for over a week and whitied over the pile of dishes in the sink. I went back to bed and wiped my mouth on the pillowcase.

Dad screamed, "Yid bitter fuckin clean those dishes ye wir sick oan, ya fat wee bitch." So I did, but the water wasn't hot and with no Fairy liquid the smell got worse. Scooping the chunky bits out made me vomit again, but I was clever and avoided the sink and it landed on the floor with a splat.

Dad went mental and hit me with a flipflop, but I blocked his second whack, as I learned karate from this late-night TV show and kicked him in the face. He fell and smashed his head on the sink and landed in my watery sick. He did that thing that the Undertaker does with his eyes and made them all white and blood ran from his head. I mopped around him with my socks so when he woke up there wouldn't be any mess and he'd not be angry and forgive me and maybe buy me some of those melon laces from the Co-op I like.

After three days, Dad hadn't moved, so I borrowed his big puffy jacket and workie boots and got on the 42 bus to nowhere and sat on the top deck beside a heater. Mum called saying she wouldn't be able to take me again this weekend. I said okay and Dad was sleeping but I'd let him know. I closed my eyes, mouth watering, wishing I'd never eaten that curry.

On the Road Again

Florence Flannigan

"That's me away son, be back around tea time with your favourite steak pie."

"Bye Dad," shouts Seamus.

Hopefully the roads are clear, and I can get to Cumbernauld in ten minutes, thinks Ricky. He flips over his Irn Bru factory lanyard and covers the tired face staring back at him. "Oh, lights are changing, GUTTY DOWN… what the feck happened there?!"

Sitting in his car, surrounded by fog, Ricky thinks he might be dead. He peers out the window, hoping the Grim Reaper will be long gone as he always had a fear of meeting that one. *Maybe it's Lucifer who is coming for me, but there's no sign of that big fucker either.* Ricky is relieved. *It's God, that's it, God who's coming. I'll be happy to see my wee mammy again. But what about my wee boy? He'd be an orphan…*

After a long while, nobody appears, so Ricky gets out of the car.

"Hello?"

"Hey mate, you here long?" a voice shouts back. "I've been here since, well, quite a while now, years it seems. I was trampin along the bypass then BOOM."

"I was skelpin home through traffic then, just want to go home now," another voice says.

"We think it's the cars they're after."

Ricky is baffled. *The cars? Could have nicked them any time, why bring the drivers here?* He thinks about what the others said: *'trampin along', 'skelpin through'* and realises he had put the *'gutty down'*.

Speeding that's it, we were all speeding and at that, he was back on the road again heading for Cumbernauld.

The Ballad of the Moon Dogs

C.W. O'Sullivan

Her eyes dripped like honey as the wind painted with a haunted brush. She watched the spot between the two larger dead sycamore trees that was rumoured to house the mythical moon dogs.

"Out with ye, peasants!" she screamed. She couldn't be out past ten or the master's door would be locked; sleeping in the decaying undergrowth was no place for a girl made of shimmering glass.

The moon dogs appeared, inhaling the air – she clapped and clapped as more and more came out. They were real! They were real! With an open rucksack she sprinted around the field, sweeping up the dogs like butterflies until her bag was bursting at the seams and ran inside to the kitchen.

"Endangered no more, last of yer kind. Intae our soup ye go, don't be fraid oh no hot water ye pittance of a creatures."

Once the pot warmed, she took off her clothes and climbed into the water. She pulled in the bag of dogs.

"Ah thinks we needs some pepper!" They seemed confused but soon began to swim and play. She laughed. They licked her face;

their fear had evaporated. The water got hotter and hotter. She closed her eyes and planned to sleep right through it. Then she screamed and panicked. She tried to get out and knocked over the pot. The water went everywhere. The moon dogs all dead; her skin all but gone.

A servant girl screamed when she saw all the dead rats. The master came in with his musket, saw his only child: he shot her in the head then shot himself.

All Deals are Final

Colin Burnett

"You want me tae become a loan shark?" Craig asks, horrified at the mere suggestion. "Ah dunno, Aldo. Nae offence but ah've no goat the hert fur that line ae work."

"People borrae a quid and we chairge fiver," ah educate him. "Dinnae worry, eh? Hings rarely git messy. Nae bairns are ever hermed. Wur no fuckin animals. As fur wumen, though? We decide oan a case tae case basis."

Ah continue wae this sales pitch.

"Aw yae need tae dae is kick back and watch the money flow in. Hink ae it as a public service. So, what dae yae say?"

"Ah'll talk it through wae Christine and see what she hinks," his jumpy voice vents.

"Dougie wis right, then?"

"Aboot what?"

"Ah wis roond his place the other day. Yur name came up and words wur exchanged. Apparently, yur a bawless fud who cannae take a forward step withoot Christine giein yae the nod first. Dougie's words, no mine. Ah telt him Craigy's a man who kens his ain mind but clearly ah must stand corrected."

Noo that the fuse is lit ah sit back and watch him perform the back stroke. Truth is ah've no clapped eyes oan Dougie in a fortnight.

"Cheeky bastard! Ah'm the man ae ma hoose. Ma word is final."

"Ah've alweys said we're cut fae a different cloth fae that Great Gatsby wannabee. Sure, we might be anchored doon by the auld baw and chain. But we answer tae naeone. Kin ah take that as yur oanboard?"

"Aye," he says as he reaches oor the desk tae gee me a hearty handshake.

Col and He's Seen People Die

Douglas Bruton

People die in movies sometimes. Col has seen that. Someone shot and falling from a horse, landing in the dirt. Mostly there's no blood but it's understood they've died. Every Saturday morning on the big screen at the Odeon, price sixpence.

And once he saw an old man lying in the street next to a crushed bicycle. A woman loosened his collar and an urgent younger man was talking to him. The old man's eyes were closed; if you looked, you could see he was not breathing. Col should've felt something then but he wasn't sure what.

Then came a night his parents went out to a dance – Mum dressed in a yellow swing dress, Dad scrubbed up clean as a new penny. Col was told to take himself off to bed at the usual time, about nine o'clock. But he didn't. Instead, he watched the TV with the sound turned down. That's when he saw it.

On the news, a grainy clip of a black-and-white film, a boy kneeling, hands tied behind his back, his face crumpled and creased and pleading. A man in a uniform holding him with one hand, in the other hand a gun. Then, without warning so there was not time to look away, the man put the gun quick to the boy's head, pulled the trigger. With the sound turned down you couldn't hear the shot, but the boy's head jerked a little and all his body went slack – that's how you knew.

Col switched the TV off. He felt something then – a fearful shaking as he snatched for breath. Col and he's seen people die.

Biped Unperceived

M. J. Nicholls

Prior to the ritual bowling of breakfast muesli, an argument erupted in the lift of the Butch Wilmore Moonwalk Memorial Hotel. A complex and unloving clamour had emerged from Room 274 the previous e'en, causing sleepless agitation in the neighbouring suites. The noise began as a sweet-natured swoosh (couscous flowing into a mason jar), then a flutter of violent sputters (the exhaust backfiring of a Renault Espace), building to a frantic fast-fisted outrage (the shock of two beef shanks being carved in manic concurrence).

Lasting nineteen minutes, the noise kept the occupants of rooms 275 and 276 awake across a night of torturous tossing with additional turning when required. A buff divorcée with a retouched philtrum named Karaline said the noise brought to mind the cooing of a carrion crow in a state of high priapic dudgeon, while a beardless artisan pizzamaker named Britchlee said the noise reminded him of a cooked chicken being throttled through the innards of a Bösendorfer piano. The third lift occupant, a stubble-shanked economist named Meredith, said the noise was akin to a pencil being shorn in the corner of a Louis VII armoire.

The arguing increased in volume and pitch and timbre and ugliness until it attained such a throb of consensuslessness clamour no one noticed when the lift opened and the occupant of Room 274 strolled past pulling a triple-horned biped of unknown origin or species in a cage – silent on passing, later expected to be somewhat disruptive in another hotel in another city, causing sleepless nights to another three random people for another unknown reason in another unwritten story of approximately or exactly specifically 274 words.

Byre

Margaret Elphinstone

The farmhouse walls have been taken back to honey-coloured stone: the kitchen's now a sitting room – woven rugs, sofas, and tasteful pottery. Would the farm women – four centuries of them – appreciate this shabby-chic? The inglenook's still black from ancient smoke.

Dinner over, my host escorts me down the hollowed outside stairs to my room: "It's the original byre. You're the first to stay in it."

I step into dimness: white counterpaned bed, carved table, reading lamp. A moonlit view to a snaking ridge, red soil dotted with maquis. Thyme scents rise from the cobbles. I open the window to the stars and fall into bed.

Listen!

No!

Hands reach

Thicker than dark

Can't breathe

No!

Trembling, I switch on the light. White walls, ceiling, curtains. Pure white. I breathe deeply. Switch off the light.

No!

Can't breathe

Please God

Not this

No!

I shove the bed from the back wall to the open doors and lie as close to outdoors as possible.

Come morning I put everything back. I say nothing.

That night I lie down. There's nothing wrong. I switch off the light.

No!

God have mercy

No!

Not this

I push the bed again to the open doorway. At last sleep steals across the cobbles.

Vichy France!

I sit upright. *Vichy France.* The far ridge is outlined in moonlight, a faint line of script across the parchment sky. There isn't much about Vichy France in my guidebook. It's been mentioned only once – by the old man who holds the church keys. Our hostess mentioned where we were staying. "Vichy France," he said, looking past us. Somewhere else.

The Porcelain Orchestra

Kirsti Wishart

Some rooms of the museum were so rarely visited the atmosphere had become uncanny. Guards experienced a disturbing switch, felt as if they were the ones on display, the objects watching and studying. Hallucinations started, a guard found in the Glass Hall staring at her right hand that seemed to her transparent. When touched on the shoulder she shivered like a sheet of paper caught in a breeze, whispered, "Watch or I'll shatter." Another claimed a Meissen shepherdess had fainted when her typewritten, yellowing description label had actually been read.

A whistling night-guard who experienced no issues suggested that along with temperature and lighting controls, what was needed to maintain the health of the exhibits was love. This could be communicated not only through increased visitor numbers but by touch, provided by music's delicate vibration. So the evening concerts began.

People were sceptical but mid-way through the first event, they felt the change, a lessening of pressure. Instruments kept locked in cases were brought into literal play. Their polished wood and metal seemed to glow as they were truly appreciated rather than admired in passing. Press your hand against a cabinet and you would feel a tremor, the rococo gods decorating a Dresden platter sighing in relief.

The musicians didn't want to stop and when they did they were dazed. Although the audience was small, it was as if they'd played to thousands. And they had, to ghosts, those who made and traded, owned and been intimately involved with the exhibits. The living and the dead brought together in the rippling waves of applause, warmth filling the corridors, setting porcelain singing.

Hands on the Window

Judith Hughes

The mass of bodies at Kharkiv station seemed to suck the air from my lungs like a syringe syphoning blood. At eleven, I wasn't yet tall enough to feel the fresh air above and my head swam with the crush and the heat of layers of clothes I was forced to don that morning. I felt too old to hold my mother's hand, even if I wanted to, so I held onto a toggle of my father's army jacket. It was a crumb of comfort. My father's face was pale under the dark beard; my mother's paler still, the muscles at the side of her jaw standing out. The train was heading west away from the shelling and gunfire. Away from home. Our final destination, I was told, was a place called Scotland, a land of mountains, trees, and water. I had never heard of it.

We fought our way to a window seat in the carriage, my mother elbowing even elderly people out of the way. Our bags of belongings were dumped on the floor as we searched for my father in the sea of faces on the platform. A familiar hand appeared, and he pressed his palm to the window. I did the same, my hand almost engulfed by his with the icy window between us. He was trying to say something to us, shouting at the glass, steaming it up and obscuring his face.

"Look after your mother, Bohdan. Get on with life."

At that moment, I loathed him for making us leave.

"I hate you," I screamed at the window as the train started its journey westwards.

When Perceptions are Taken as Truth

Philip Paris

Janet is naked, although the tar covers her body more intimately than clothes ever could. It's an obscene embrace. The stench of the black, sticky mess stings her eyes and choaks her lungs. It will hug her until the end, near now, for the judge, jury, dignitaries and accusers are gathered, replenished from Dornoch's taverns where they'll return afterwards to congratulate themselves on a good job. God's work done.

The crowd screams unimaginable hate and fear despite Janet being unknown to them. She's as much a stranger as they are to her. Of course, they think they know. They perceive her to be different... and perceptions only have to be shouted often enough to be taken as truth.

The courtroom was filled with people she had never met. Some made the most extraordinary claims. According to one Janet had turned her own daughter into a pony so that she could ride around and do the Devil's bidding. Great cries of shock and horror had echoed throughout the courtroom at such evil.

Janet thought it would probably have been easier to use the real pony they had rather than turning Aila into one, but no-one asked her opinion on the matter. They wouldn't have listened, even if she'd had the chance to speak.

Aila was also meant to be executed this morning, but she escaped from the tolbooth. They won't catch her. It's Janet's one comfort as the executioner walks over, a flaming torch in his hand.

Later, people will queue up to buy him drinks.

The Prince

Shay Patrick Collins

There is a shitey bar I live above. 'Zebrados'. A small hellhole that could fit 20 odd people, but they let 50 in on a bad night just to piss me off. It is shoulder to shoulder, breathing in dirt, sweat, and sneezes. Ancient pictures of Bonnie Prince Charlie litter the walls from when it was called The Prince 20 odd years ago. But the tiny bar does have a star attraction: the angelic bartenderess, Gina Rennie.

Gina brings over my pint of cold Guinness without asking.

"There ye go, pal."

"Thank you, ma darling. You are as pretty as a picture."

"Aw, fanks, Oweny. Like him?"

She points at the Bonnie Prince looking like he's been pushed through a meat condenser.

"No that picture."

She laughs.

Sitting there every night with a freezing fireplace (never lit) by my feet, I watch and listen to the same punters come in and talk about the same pish. I'm invisible. At midnight, last orders, I finish my 8th pint and switch it up.

"Jack and Coke, Gina, darling. No ice. Easy on the coke."

It's as loud as a beehive. I sip my wumen's drink and continue to stare at Gina. Swift and always in control.

I collect a few pint empties and put them on the bar, chasing out the hanger oners.

"That's everyone away now, sweetheart."

She's in the back cashing up and gives me a wave without looking up.

"You want tae go for a kebab? A right good one?"

She ignores me – that was a mistake. Should have locked the door. I move in behind her and she's already greeting.

Here Come the Strike Pilots

Charles McGarry

They found the strike pilot hanging from the high perimeter of an electrical substation, his tangled chute snagged upon the spiked railings and then draped over the inside of the fence and then two ugly grey power transformers. His feet dangled about two metres from the ground, his helmeted head at a sickeningly unnatural angle, his gloved hands facing slightly outwards in an attitude of astonishment, or perhaps the opposite of that, perhaps one of submission to death.

Two of Lightbody's men had heard the faint, high-altitude, transonic gushing sound and looked up to see the raking contrails of a squadron in solemnly dogged, textbook formation. Likely they had the oilfields to the northwest in their sights. Perhaps the pilot had bailed out due to a mechanical malfunction, and his neck been broken either during the ejector seat's deployment or when he had struck the fence.

Everyone stood transfixed by the hanging figure, his scuffed flying boots moving almost imperceptibly from side to side as the paracords creaked, his flight helmet, black visor and respirator lending him an alien countenance. There was an unspoken energy of hatred among the onlookers, a hatred rooted in the fear which had grown in the ranks towards strike pilots and their deadly turbojet fighter-bombers, to which they were almost entirely vulnerable. Their hatred was edged with envy, envy for the generally superior technology of the enemy, so when Private Ellis, who was an aviation bore, piped up with the likely model of the deceased man's machine, it drew dirty looks.

"He's lucky he wasn't electrocuted," continued Ellis, oblivious.

"Lucky? He's bleedin' dead anyway," countered Private Oakley.

The Astronaut

Jack McInnes

Jimmy sealed the helmet and stared. A Russian astronaut suit, but it had been in actual space. Well worth £32.50 from the jumble sale. Gave his reflection a thumbs-up and walked out the bathroom.

"I'm off, Betty."

"Okay, have fun."

Jimmy waded across the field behind his garden, remembering the '69 Moon landing. Only meant to work in the factory for a year to save up. Yes, it had been over 50 years but wasn't too late. Armstrong, Aldrin, Kirk, Picard – knew them all. Heard his neighbours laughing over the fence.

"What do they know?"

He grabbed the Saltire and planted it in the crater. In five weeks, he was going to NASA.

"Wow. Jimmy McIntyre is super fit. 70? No way. He's 45 at the very most – around the same age we sent Armstrong. Get him on that fucking spaceship."

Jimmy pictured kissing his wife goodbye and waving at the grandchildren. The moon? Mars? Pluto? Prepared for them all.

"You want a sausage?" Betty said as he arrived at the back door.

"What did I tell you – no rubbish."

"Oh okay."

Jimmy slumped in his chair and sighed. By the time he had finished polishing his visor, his mouth watered.

"Can I smell kippers?"

"The van brought them yesterday."

"Fine, I'll do another ten minutes then I can enjoy it."

Jimmy made it back to the Moon but felt strange. Must have been the smell of that delicious fish trapped inside.

"Houston, I'm having technical proble—" He clutched his chest, and the field spun, fading to static. Saw an outline of Betty rushing towards him as the ashy afternoon glow turned molten.

Flea Market

Tony Garner

Since he'd been on his own, he'd got better at talking about his emotions, but there were still things he'd never admit. One was he liked to take his daughter places where she'd see things from his world.

They strolled along the alleys of the antique dealers. Men and women sitting in front of their gilt furniture, oil paintings, leonine statuettes, chewing their politicians to shreds, secure in their world of dealing in the past.

Inside, up some stairs, stalls selling books, LPs, CDs, even cassettes, the owners with faces like old actors, cigarettes tucked into the corners of their mouths. He flicked through some LPs – Serge Gainsbourg, France Gall, your mother and I used to listen to – as he hoped, she sighed, wandered away.

They moved to the edgier margins, scrappier stalls, sellers from the former colonies. She was offered sunglasses, him watches, all blatant knock-offs. Clothes within her teenage budget, 20 euros, 15. If the price isn't there just ask, c'est combien? He demonstrated. She wandered on. Good.

He kept a distance, watching his daughter surrounded by racks of black leather jackets like subway pickpockets. Stealing glances from behind fake football shirts – pleased to see her fingering the jackets, stretching out, taking one off the rack. Go on, he willed her. He saw her glance at the owner talking to another guy in Arabic. You don't need to ask, just do it. But timidity got the better of her, and she put it back. She turned, looking for him, no longer in command of the jackets, instead hounded by them and what they represented – her mother, as she used to be.

A Red Lipstick Kind of Day

Anne Hamilton

It's dark when I wake; I can see stars through the skylight. We have a conservatory, decking, and even a koi pond – well, why shouldn't those of us eeking out our dying days do so in pretty surroundings?

My hair's the colour of the sky as it lightens. It looks better on the sky: a monochrome palette, storm-laden grey to light white, not the colourless wisps shredding on to my pillow. Darren, the nurse who, as the young ones say, *gets me*, comes over and we look up together.

"Definitely a glad rags and fake-it-til-you-make-it kind of day, Nancy," he decides. Ignoring the drip stand, the obs sheets, and Matron's lips (forever pursed-up like a Manx cat's arse), he holds the mirror while I get my wig on. "Fluff the blonde bits out more," he orders, adding, "Subtle but determined. I like it," as I top up my eyebrows and risk a smudge of blue eye-shadow. Above us, the sun inches out, blueing the sky, too.

"Cracking, darlin'," Darren says.

Matron, who's behind the flimsy curtain, mopping up the mess that's my neighbour, Martina, clears her throat.

Darren winks at me and raises his voice. "Sun's out, fun's out, Nancy. Sure, let's leave your dying to a day that's already feckin' miserable. Hold out for February, can ye? That shite bit when we all want to top ourselves."

Matron stops rattling Martina's pills and snorts. Darren gives her the finger, which gives me the pep to reach for my make-up bag again.

Today might even be a slash of bright red lipstick kind of day.

Trail Dust

Stephanie Garcia

The sun shining on the tops of their heads.

You're small. And everyone older than you, if only by months, is like a Goliath. Even your mother seems to have gigantic hands, no matter how delicate.

The place didn't really matter; it just always felt more like flying when outside.

Even if the outside was a parking lot.

They had you sandwiched, but you would usually never ask straightforward for it. Instead, there would be the big copper pot staring eyes, a tug on the shirt. Or a clasp of both their hands at once, equipped with the smallest sprint forward you could muster.

They would give in; this couldn't go on for years. 1, 2, 3…

And then with all their parental strength they would hoist you up and in reverse, so that your body would be parallel to the surface beneath you. Eyes closed, the wind in your ears seems to delay time.

Again, again, you say.

We sit, legs loose. The table leaning more toward me, and we both know I'm more likely to spill. Especially pints. One, two, three. Not a dribble escapes our mouths. Just words about situations that should be Sunday morning comic strips or things that go bump in the night. Talking in all caps for emphasis, making those hand gestures like Americans do, while we flash our pearly whites in-between the punch lines, the sips. You tell a real classic, your last one. And as my hand slows down to wipe the wet patches around my eyes, I look up and there's a white line in the sky.

We Shall Speak in Whispers

Dòmhnall Gall

The cold mountain was thick with relief when they dug Father out of the snow after eight long days. His hands were green and sandy, his teeth were missing, and grey face covered in scratch marks. But he was alive. I felt something was off but put that down to the overwhelming emotions of finding him. The other five in his group were nowhere to be found.

That night at the hospital, Mum and Eilidh were delighted as Father joked and told of his strange climb up Ben Nevis and the freak blizzard that caught them all off guard. Of how he was blown off the side, away from the others, and managed to keep his spirits up in his burrow by thinking about his family. Mum squeezed his hand and wiped her eyes. Beyond a miracle he made it off that mountain. The doctors said he could even go home in a few days. It was the last time he was ever leaving Inverness again he promised and laughed.

The boy waited until they left to get some tea and sat by the bed. Father picked at his fingernails and tore his pinky one in half and held it up to the bedside lamp. He took out a cup of motor oil and drank it. It dripped over his chin and into the coarse black hairs on his chest.

"Who are you?" the boy asked, eyes brimming.

Father picked at a scab on his lip and ate it.

"Does it matter?"

Father

Coinneach MacIntyre

Hebridean fruit stained his fingers; the days in the fields are now over.

"Whit ye gonna dae now, Da?"

You are an only child, but he never answers. The autumnal winds are sold to winter and turn bitter. Together, you watch foreign men cut down birch trees as you hum the words of a song you've heard a thousand times but never quite learned.

"Whit wull we dae if oh the trees ir massa-curd?"

"Their blood runs through yir veins, gurl, they'll niver die, as long as yir true."

Winter turns to summer like a clap. You are afraid to stand under those satin waterfalls until he holds your shoulders.

"If ah fell in wud ah die?"

"They wud bend ye like a box. But we don't die, no really. Whits important never dies. De ye believe in the spirits that shaped the mountains?"

Summer breaks like a biscuit. Bathe in dirt water in a bucket by the peat fire, mother singing A Mhairead Òg.

"Ma, why de ye mend books no one wull ever read?"

"Small things must be mended before we can see the bigger picture," Mirren.

"De ye miss Da?"

"Your father is where he is meant to be."

"We niver foun his body. He cud still be oot there."

You never give up hope of seeing him again. How can you?

At midnight you pray.

"Where did ye go? Ah deserve tae know!"

You are no longer a child. But he never answers.

When You Comin Back?

Callum McSorley

You know the beer over there is just synthetic pish.

"It's an acquired taste."

And the eggs don't come fae chickens.

"I only ever have them scrambled. I wouldn't know anyway."

You'll be wearin one of those big suits then, will you? And the hings on your feet.

"My Sunday attire."

And that's another one. Church. You can't still be goin to church over there. Surely not. They wouldn't allow it, would they. Can't stand a Cathlic. Cannot stand a Cathlic over there. They'll have you up on a cross yourself. So they will.

"I'm not Cathlic."

It doesn't matter, it's just an example. There's no tolerance is what I mean. Not like here. And what are you gonna do on Friday, Seturday nights? The boays, the tunes, the madness. Moan to fuck, man, it'll be borin. You'll be bored. Work, sleep, work, sleep, work, sleep. Eat and shite too if you're lucky. Neither of which will involve solids, I tell you that for fuck all.

"They have drugs that can help your gut adjust."

And what about your bones. The density. Your spine. They got drugs for that and aw? Couldn't pay me to go through that. Could not pay me. And the poor buggers, the natives, they don't get paid much, do they? It's awright for you swannin over there and makin a packet. Hoose paid for. Expenses covered. Tax free. Expat privileges.

They've got the death penalty. Explosive decompression. That's what they do. Lock you in the chamber then flush you away like a turd.

"Aye, for murderers. I'm not plannin on killin anybody."

So you say now.

Please don't go.

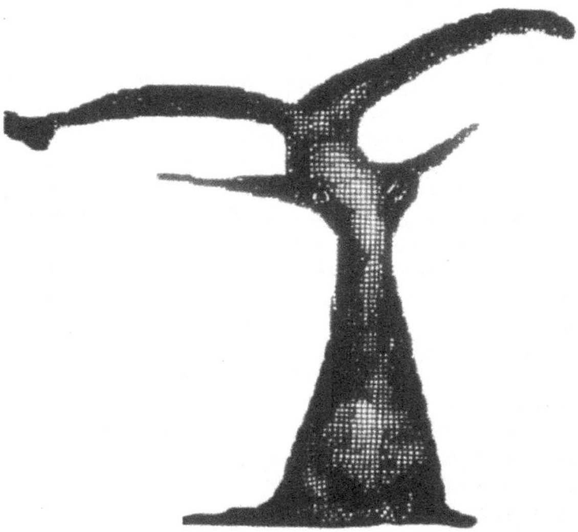

Contributors

Lisa Ballantyne is the internationally bestselling author of five novels. Her debut, The Guilty One was nominated for an Edgar Allan Poe Award, Longlisted for the International IMPAC Dublin Literary Award and the Theakston Old Peculiar Crime Novel of the Year Award, and was also a Richard and Judy Book Club bestseller. Her second novel, Good Bad Love, (published as Everything She Forgot in America) was a USA Today bestseller. She has been a Robert Louis Stevenson Fellow in France, supported by Scottish Book Trust and Creative Scotland. Her work has been translated into nearly thirty languages. Her most recent novel is The Innocent One, published in 2023. Born in Armadale, West Lothian, she now lives in Glasgow.

Gordon Brown (aka Morgan Cry) has twelve novels published to date. His latest The Cost is the start of a new crime series set in the northeast of Scotland. The sequel, The Fracture, will be published on the 4th of November. Gordon is a founding member of Bloody Scotland, is married with two children (grown up), and was once booed by 49,000 people while on the pitch of a major football cup final.

Ricky Monahan Brown's memoir, Stroke: A 5% chance of survival, was a Scotsman Nonfiction Book of 2019. The spoken word event he co-founded, Interrobang?! won the 2017 Saboteur Award for Best Regular Spoken Word Night in Britain. His novella Little Apples is available from Leamington Books and his fiction collection, Terminal, was published by sincere corkscrew in autumn 2024.

Douglas Bruton's short stories and flash fictions have won many competitions including with Fish and The Neil Gunn Prize. His children's novel, The Chess Piece Magician was published by Floris Books (2009); his literary fiction debut, Mrs Winchester's Gun Club, was published by Scotland Street Press (2019); Blue Postcards, longlisted for the Walter Scott Prize for Historical Fiction 2022, and With or Without Angels (2023) and Woman in Blue (2025) were all published by Fairlight Books; a novella called Just Like Him To Die was published by Leamington Books (2022); and Taproot Press published Hope Never Knew Horizon (2024).

Colin Burnett (36) from Bonnyrigg has written two novels A Working Class State of Mind and Who's Aldo. He's written extensively for newspapers and has been nominated for Scots Media Person of the Year (2021) and Scots Writer of the Year (2022). Also, recently he was featured in the List magazines annual Hot100 of Scotland's most influential creatives (2024).

Rachel Carmichael lives in Glasgow. Her stories have appeared in thi wurd magazine, thi wurd's anthology Alternating Current, Northwords Now, NFFD's flash flood, the Federation of Writers Scotland 2020 anthology, and New Writing Scotland.

Phillip Clark is a graphic novel and book illustrator from Moodiesburn, North Lanarkshire.

Shay Patrick Collins was born in Glasgow. When he's not writing short stories, you'll find him bagging Munros with his dog, Sean and wife and editor, Diane. He has published twelve short stories and is working on his debut novel, which this short story The Prince is an extract from.

Seamus Connolly is relatively new to the Scottish literary scene and the author of two crime thriller novels, Black is the Colour and Death Before Revenge. Both are set in Paisley in the 1980's and capture the heartache, humour and resilience and spirit of a community decimated by Thatcher's de-industrialisation policies while taking the reader on a journey with many twists and turns. Seamus was born and brought up in Paisley by his Irish parents and continues to live locally.

Ross Crawford is a scriever/writer based in Stirling, working in Scots and English. He was awarded a 2024 New Writers Award from the Scottish Book Trust for his work in Scots. His work has been published by Speculative Books, Eemis Stane, Lallans, and Soor Ploom Press among others. You can find his website at www.rrmcrawford.com

John Dean is a best-selling crime novelist living in Dumfries and Galloway, who has had twenty five novels published by The Book Folks, which recently became a Joffe Books company. He is the creator of the DCI John Blizzard and DCI Jack Harris series. John is the Crime Writers' Association's Libraries Champion in Scotland and was the founder of the annual Kirkcudbright Book Week literary festival in South West Scotland.

Margaret Elphinstone began her writing career in the 1980s with two futuristic fantasy novels. More recently she has turned from writing mainly historical novels (e.g. The Sea Road, Voyageurs) to addressing the existential crises of our times through a Mesolithic novel The Gathering Night, poetry, short stories and her novella, Lost People, shortlisted for a 2024 Saltire Award. She is Professor Emerita of Writing at Strathclyde University.

John Gerard Fagan is the author of the memoir Fish Town (2021) and the historical fiction novel Silent Riders of the Sea (2024). He has over 100 short stories published in places such as Deus Ex Machina, thi wurd, and Black Static. As an Assistant Professor, he has taught Literature, Creative Writing, and Academic English, and worked at universities across the world, including The University of Edinburgh, Herriot Watt University, and Meikai University.

Michael Anthony Fagan writes propulsive, off-beat micro-fiction short stories. A Media and English Teacher with an MA in English Literature, MLitt in Creative Writing, MA in Screenwriting, and a PDGE in Secondary Education, his award-winning work has appeared in several publications, including 42 Stories anthology, Vine Leaves Press, and Blink Ink.

Florence Flannigan is a former nurse from Glasgow who has written one novel and is writing her second, inspired by her time in Glasgow's hospitals and psychiatric wards in the 1970s/80s.

Dòmhnall Gall is from Inverness who lives and works in Glasgow. He is working on a Gaelic collection of horror set in the Scottish Highlands. We Only Speak in Whispers is a translation of an extract from the collection.

Stephanie Garcia is a writer working in communications. She has an MFA in Creative Writing from the University of Glasgow. Originally from the United States, she has spent the last 17 years making Glasgow her home, which has influenced the nostalgic tones in her writing. She is a dedicated dog mom, runs a home bakery, and enjoys and strong flat white.

Tony Garner's debut novel The Hotel Hokusai came out in February 2024 with Ringwood Publishing. He lives in Glasgow and is currently working on short fiction and a second novel.

Alan Gillespie is a writer and teacher from Fife, Scotland. His articles and stories have appeared in The New York Times, The Guardian, The Herald, Northwords Now, and New Writing Scotland. In 2011 he was awarded the Scottish Emerging Writer's residency at Cove Park. His first novel, The Mash House, was shortlisted for the Crime Writers' Association New Dagger Award 2022 for best debut.

J. Grobbelaar is a teacher who has worked and lived all over the globe. Nowadays, she lives in Glasgow with her husband, daughter, and nine-year-old Vizsla. When she has a free moment, she loses herself in her imaginary worlds, where magic wielders have adventures with dragons and other fascinating creatures.

Anne Hamilton is an author, editor and Creative Writing tutor who lives in Edinburgh. Her first book, a travel memoir titled A Blonde Bengali Wife (2010) was based on her experiences in Bangladesh and inspired the charity Bhola's Children. Her debut novel The Almost Truth (Legend Press 2024) was the winner of the Irish Novel Fair, arising from a short story in the Edinburgh Charity anthology, The People's City (Birlinn 2022) Anne's second novel Letters from Elena will be published in the summer (Legend Press 2025).

Alan Hay is a fiction writer from Dumbarton, Scotland. He writes about the outsiders – the characters who populate the fringes of society – and is influenced by the lean, concise prose of Hemingway, Carver etc. He is working towards an MA in Creative Writing at Lancaster University and is currently based in Blackpool, Lancashire. He is married, with four children, and a Dachshund.

Michele Hinchliffe grew up in Oban but regularly visited her family in Caldercruix, a small former mining village in North Lanarkshire. This piece was inspired by one of her grandmother Maisie's stories. Michele has worked in a range of jobs over the years, from graphic design to social care. She has spent the past ten years home educating her two children and is now finding time to write again. When she isn't at her laptop she can usually be found walking her dog on the Ayrshire coast or in the Atlantic hanging out with the seals.

Judith Hughes is 62 and has lived in Scotland for nearly 14 years, firstly in Fife and now by the shores of Loch Tay. Mountains, water, and the outdoors are my things. She had a career in Medicine, for which she had to leave, behind formal study of literature and the arts. Now, on retirement, she has returned to this and is immensely enjoying writing stories.

Coinneach MacIntyre is a poet, wildlife photographer, and fisherman originally from Glasgow who lives in Wellington with his wife and four daughters, and one granddaughter. In his spare time, he occasionally lectures on the works of Tolkien. Father is his first published fictional piece of work.

Charles McGarry was born in Glasgow in 1972 and has lived most of his life in Scotland. His fiction is mostly set in Scotland and often celebrates the landscapes and culture of the country. He co-wrote The Road to Lisbon with Martin Greig (Birlinn, 2012), and since 2017 has had three critically acclaimed Leo Moran murder mysteries published by Polygon and BackPage as Charles E McGarry: The Ghost of Helen Addison, The Shadow of the Black Earl, and The Mystery of the Strange Piper. His latest novel, A Solemn Stillness Holds, a post-apocalyptic adventure set in near-future Scotland, is out now.

Jack McInnes is originally from the Southside of Glasgow, emigrating to Melbourne, Australia in 2006. He has been writing fiction since he retired as a joiner and lives with his dog Rodger. He writes flash fiction primarily set in Scotland or Australia.

Liam McLeod is a Glaswegian short story writer and zine maker who splits his time between his native city and Belfast and his writing is influenced more than anything by his upbringing in the East End. You can find him hill walking, seeking inspiration, or in the pub washing the day away.

Rob McClure is a Scottish writer albeit currently expatriate. He has published short fiction in Gutter, Chapman, Warwick Review, Barcelona Review, Manchester Review, and many such magazines, and won the Black Springs Crime Fiction Prize for a novel called The Scotsman (Black Springs Press, 2023).

Callum McSorley is a writer based in Glasgow whose short stories have appeared in Gutter Magazine, Shoreline of Infinity, and New Writing Scotland. His debut novel, Squeaky Clean – a crime thriller inspired by his years working at a car wash in Glasgow's East End – was published in 2023. With it, Callum became the youngest ever author to win the prestigious McIlvanney Prize for best Scottish Crime novel of the year and gathered critical acclaim from The Times, The Scotsman, the Wall Street Journal, and more. His second novel, Paperboy, is out now.

Iain Allan Mills was born in Bellshill in 1977. He grew up in East Kilbride and studied a music undergrad in Scotland and philosophy postgrad in Wales. He has lived all over the UK and is now quite settled in the Welsh Valleys. He is also the author of Relaxing Music for Dogs and If we think in terms of invisible geometrics.

M. J. Nicholls lives in Glasgow. His most recent novel is The Fall and Fall of Derek Haffman.

C.W. O'Sullivan is a Scottish travel writer who has lived all over the world, calling many cities home: from Copenhagen, Malmo, Berlin and Prague to Tokyo, Los Angeles, and Perth. He currently resides in Edinburgh where he reads his short stories to his two cats.

Philip Paris lives in the Highlands and much of his work is inspired by Scottish history. His novel, The Last Witch of Scotland, is Waterstones Scottish Book of the Year 2024. His forthcoming historical fiction, A Fire in Their Hearts, which was inspired by the 17th century Scottish Covenanters, will be published on 28th August 2025. When Perceptions are Taken as Truth is based on true events.

Janet Horne died in June, 1727, the last person in Britain to be executed for witchcraft.

Kate Peel is a Creative Writing student. Her writing often features unique, and slightly magical, encounters with nature and animals. Originally from Canada, Kate 'came home' to Scotland and lives on the Clyde coast with her partner and their Golden Retriever.

Anjali Ramayya, inspired by life in India and Scotland, the two countries she calls home, started writing poetry and short fiction following retirement from a career in psychiatry and medical software development. Her work has been listed and placed in competitions, including Scottish Association of Writers and Plough. Her poetry has been published by Poetry Scotland, Propel, Dreich, Soor Ploom, Writers' Umbrella, and Mirrorball, as well as anthologies including Ukraine – A World Anthology of Poems on War, Short and Sweet volume 2 by Soor Ploom Press, and thi wurd's 2024 anthology Earthy Rewards.

Dickson Telfer works part-time in education teaching academic literacies and spend the remainder involved in: writing, editing, proofreading, publishing, writing/performing music, and hosting events. Author of the short-story collections The Red Man Turns to Green and Refrigerator Cake. Co-author of The Lives of Reilly, a memoir about former professional footballer Mark 'Mavis' Reilly. Published in various litzines and anthologies. Part of the team at Razur Cuts, which includes running the not-for-profit book publishing arm and its parent company, Nameless Town.

Douglas Thompson is a former Chair and Director of the Scottish Writers Centre and has published more than 20 novels and collections of short stories and poetry from various publishers in the UK, Europe and the Americas, including The Brahan Seer from Acair Books (2014) and most recently Retrovival from Elsewhen Press (2025). He won the Herald/Grolsch Question Of Style Award in 1989, 2nd prize in the Neil Gunn Writing Competition 2007, and the Faith/Unbelief Poetry Prize in 2016. His short story The Dissolving Man is on the reading list of the Edinburgh University contemporary Scottish fiction course.

www.douglasthompson.wordpress.com

LG Thomson was born in Glasgow, grew up in Cumbernauld, and went to art school in Dundee. She now lives in the Highlands. Her writing has appeared in a wide range of literary magazines and anthologies and she is the author of seven novels, including neo noir thriller, Boyle's Law. Her latest books, Modernist Dreams Brutalist Nightmares and Bitter Fruit (Outcast Press) are darkly funny memoirs about growing up in Scotland in the 1970s and 1980s. Find out more at www.LGThomson.com

Thomas Welsh is a narrative director and novelist. He was lead writer and narrative director on Cloudpunk and City of Ghosts and is currently working on Nivalis and Best Served Cold. He has written for numerous game sites including Kotaku, has several short stories in print, has presented a talk at GDC, and works with The Scottish Book Trust with their Live Literature Programme, where he talks at Schools and Libraries. He is the author of the Metiks Fade Trilogy, and is teaching Games Narrative at the Glasgow School of Art.

Kirsti Wishart lives and works in Edinburgh. Her short stories have appeared in New Writing Scotland, the Glasgow Review of Books, and Product. Her new novel, The Pocketbook Guide to Scottish Superheroes, will soon appear serialised via the SF Caledonia website.

Tantallon Tìr

www.tantallontir.com